STERLING CHILDREN'S BOOKS
New York

An Imprint of Sterling Publishing
387 Park Avenue South
New York, NY 10016

STERLING CHILDREN'S BOOKS and the distinctive Sterling Children's Books
logo are trademarks of Sterling Publishing Co., Inc.

© 2014 by Sterling Publishing Co, Inc

ISBN 978-1-4027-8347-0

Distributed in Canada by Sterling Publishing
c/o Canadian Manda Group, 165 Dufferin Street
Toronto, Ontario, Canada M6K 3H6
Distributed in the United Kingdom by GMC Distribution Services
Castle Place, 166 High Street, Lewes, East Sussex, England BN7 1XU
Distributed in Australia by Capricorn Link (Australia) Pty. Ltd.
P.O. Box 704, Windsor, NSW 2756, Australia

For information about custom editions, special sales, and premium
and corporate purchases, please contact Sterling Special Sales at
800-805-5489 or specialsales@sterlingpublishing.com.

Manufactured in China
Lot #:
2 4 6 8 10 9 7 5 3 1
08/14

www.sterlingpublishing.com/kids

SILVER PENNY STORIES

The Lion and the Mouse

Told by Kathleen Olmstead
Illustrated by Scott Wakefield

One day, a lion was taking a nap. He was lying in the shade of a great big tree.

A tiny mouse came by. Seeing the sleeping lion, he decided to play. He crawled up the lion's leg and onto his back.

The mouse ran up and down the lion's back. He ran onto the lion's head. He ran down the lion's front leg.

As the mouse was running to the lion's other leg, a great paw caught him. The lion was awake!

The lion picked up the mouse and he opened his mouth wide. Suddenly, a tiny voice said, "Stop! Please!"

It was the mouse. "Please, Great Lion," he said. "I am sorry I woke you up."

The lion closed his mouth. He held the mouse while he listened.

"Please let me go," the mouse begged.

"I will not forget your kindness.

Maybe, one day I can help you."

The lion laughed. What could a mouse do to help him? Still, the mouse was brave to ask.

The lion let the mouse go. As the little mouse ran away, he said, "Thank you! I will never forget you."

The lion went back to sleep. When he woke up from his long nap, the lion had forgotten all about the mouse.

A long time passed. The lion was taking another nap under the same tree. This time, it was not a mouse that surprised him. It was hunters!

The hunters sneaked up behind the lion. They threw a rope around his neck. The lion tried to run away, but the hunters pulled the rope tight.

They put the lion in a cage made of wood. It was held together by thick rope. The lion tried to break free, but the cage was too strong.

By night, the lion had given up all hope. He lay down and closed his eyes. He could not sleep. He was very scared.

Suddenly, the lion heard something strange. It sounded like chewing. He opened his eyes. There was a little mouse nibbling on the rope.

"Hello, Lion," the mouse said quickly. He was very busy chewing the rope. He chewed through one knot then moved to the next.

One by one, the mouse chewed through the knots. The rope fell to the ground. The wooden bars fell down next. The whole cage fell down. The lion was free.

The lion was amazed. "Thank you," he said.

Then the lion recognized him. It was the little mouse he had set free.

"I promised I would help you one day," the mouse said. "Long ago, you saved me. Today, I saved you." The lion waved as the mouse ran away.

The lion learned an important lesson that day. It does not matter if someone is big or small. Anyone can show great kindness.